This LADYBIRD TALE
belongs to

....

Aladdin

Retold by Marie Stuart
with illustrations by Kou Lan

LADYBIRD 🐞 TALES

LONG AGO, IN CHINA, there lived a poor tailor named Mustafa who had a son called Aladdin.

When Mustafa fell ill and died, Aladdin's mother had to do all the work instead. Aladdin would never help.

One day, when Aladdin was out playing, a man asked him if he knew Mustafa the tailor.

"He was my father," said Aladdin, "but he is dead. Why do you ask?"

"He was my brother," the man replied. "Now that I have found you I want to help you and your mother."

"Here is some money for your mother," said Aladdin's uncle. "Tell her I will see her soon."

The next day, Aladdin saw the man again, and he invited himself to Aladdin's house for dinner.

"Here is some more money for your mother to buy something nice for us to eat," he said.

Aladdin took the money home to her.

When the man came to their house, Aladdin's mother said, "My husband never said he had a brother."

The man was not really Aladdin's uncle but a magician.

"What work do you do?" the magician asked Aladdin.

"He just plays with the other boys all day," replied Aladdin's mother.

"Then I shall buy you a shop to look after," declared the man.

Next morning, the magician took Aladdin shopping. He bought him some new clothes. The following day they went to look at big houses with lovely gardens. Aladdin liked them very much.

"One day I shall buy one," promised the magician. "But let us sit and have something to eat. We have walked a long way."

The magician fed Aladdin all the cakes and sweets he could eat. Then he said, "Let's look at the best garden of all before we go back."

When they had gone a little way, he cried, "Stop! This is the place."

The magician lit a fire with dry sticks, and put something on it that made black smoke. Then, all at once, Aladdin saw a big stone with a ring in it under his feet.

"Pull it," said the magician.

Aladdin pulled, and up came the stone. Then he saw that it had been on top of a well. It was very black inside the well and he did not like the look of it.

The magician pointed into the darkness. He said, "If you go down there and do everything I say, you will be rich."

Aladdin nodded eagerly.

"You will find a door," explained the magician. "Open it and go through. You will come to a large cave and some boxes of money. Do not take them."

"Why not?" asked Aladdin.

"Do as I say!" the magician answered angrily. Then he said, "Go on until you come to another cave, and then another. You will see boxes of gold and silver in these, but do not take any."

"When you leave the last cave, you will see a fine garden. At the end of it will be a table with a lamp on it. Bring me the lamp. You can have anything you wish from the garden," said the magician.

Then he took off a ring and gave it to Aladdin.

"This may be of use if you need help," he added. "Now go!"

Aladdin went down into the dark well. Down, down he went!

Everything was just as the magician had said. He touched nothing in any of the caves, and went through a door into the garden.

There, Aladdin found the lamp.
He took it and then looked around.
Every tree was encrusted with
rich jewels – red, blue, green, gold
and white.

Aladdin put down the lamp and
took all the jewels he could. Even
when he could carry no more,
there were still many left on
the trees.

"I shall come back again one day,"
he thought, "but now I must take
this lamp to my uncle."

So Aladdin left the garden and
went back the way he had come.

When he got to the top of the well
he could see the magician.

"Help me out, please!" Aladdin called up to him.

"Give me the lamp first," said the magician, "then you can use both hands."

But Aladdin answered, "No! Not until I get out."

The magician was very angry. He put something on the fire again and said some magic words. At once, the stone moved back into place over the well, trapping Aladdin inside.

"Wait!" he called. "I will give you the lamp if only you will help me out!"

But the magician had gone.

It was no use calling, so Aladdin tried to go back into the garden. But the door was shut tight. He sat down in the darkness and cried. For three days he had nothing to eat or drink.

"I wish I had a little fire to warm me!" he said.

He rubbed his hands and, as he did so, he rubbed the ring that the magician had given him.

"I am the slave of the ring," said a voice. "I will come whenever you rub the ring and will do anything you ask. What do you want?"

"Please take me home," begged Aladdin.

No sooner had he said this than he found that he was home!

His mother cried, "Here you are at last! I thought you were lost!"

She gave him something to eat and drink and he went to bed. The next day she said, "There is nothing left for us to eat."

But Aladdin said, "I am hungry. I shall go and see if someone will buy some of these jewels or this lamp from me."

"It looks so old," replied his mother. "Let me give it a rub first. I shall soon make it look like new. Then you will get more money for it."

Aladdin's mother took the lamp and gave it a rub. Suddenly, there was a puff of smoke, and a strange-looking man appeared. He bowed and said, "I am the slave of the lamp."

Aladdin's mother dropped the lamp in fright.

"Don't be afraid!" cried Aladdin, picking up the lamp.

Then the strange man said, "The lamp you are holding is a magic one. Whenever you rub it, I will appear and do whatever you ask."

As they were both very hungry, Aladdin said, "Please bring us something to eat and drink."

The slave of the lamp clapped his hands and a fine dinner appeared on gold plates.

When everything had been eaten, Aladdin said to his mother, "I will go to the shop and sell these plates. The money I get for them will last us a long time."

But soon that money had been spent, so Aladdin rubbed the lamp again. At once, the slave appeared and gave him everything he and his mother needed.

This went on for three or four years. By that time Aladdin was no longer a boy. He had become a man, and a very handsome one!

One day in the street, Aladdin saw a princess on horse-back and fell in love at once.

"I want to marry her," he told his mother.

"We must ask the king," she replied.

Aladdin's mother took him the last of the jewels Aladdin had found. "My son loves the princess," she said. "He sends you this gift."

"He must be a very important man!" cried the king, and he promised that Aladdin could marry the princess.

Aladdin's mother went home to tell Aladdin the good news.

But a rich man said to the king, "My son will give you much more if he can marry your daughter."

When Aladdin found this out, he rubbed the lamp.

The slave appeared and Aladdin said angrily, "Bring the princess and the rich man's son to me."

The slave did as Aladdin asked him. The man was shut in a dark room. Then Aladdin told the princess of his love for her, and how her father had promised that she could marry him.

Then the slave took her and the rich man's son back to the palace.

The rich man's son was so scared that he wouldn't marry the princess. The slave told Aladdin this. Aladdin said, "Bring me many bags of gold and jewels, and some slaves to carry them to the king."

Aladdin's mother went with the slaves, giving money to all the people on the way to the palace.

When the king looked inside the bags of gold and jewels, he cried, "Now I will let your son marry my daughter! Tell him to come here at once."

Before Aladdin went to see the king, he rubbed the lamp and said to the slave, "Bring me new clothes made of the richest cloth in the land, and a fine, white horse."

Aladdin looked just like a prince on a horse, and the princess fell in love at once.

"Before I marry her, I must have a house," said Aladdin.

That night, he rubbed the lamp and said to the slave, "Make me the best house that anyone has ever seen!"

The next morning, a beautiful house appeared, right next to the king's own palace. Aladdin married the princess, and they lived happily in their new home for a year or two. Then one day the magician came back.

When the magician found that Aladdin was alive and that he was now a prince, he was very cross.

"I must get the magic lamp away from him," he thought.

He bought some new lamps from a shop. Then he walked up and down the streets calling out, "New lamps for old! New lamps for old!"

One of the princess's women ran indoors to tell her mistress.

"Aladdin has an old lamp," thought the princess. "He will be pleased to get a new one for it."

The princess gave it to the magician in return for a new one. She planned to surprise Aladdin.

As soon as the magician had the lamp, he hid where no one could see him and gave it a rub.

The slave appeared and the magician said, "Take Aladdin's house away."

The next morning, Aladdin's house was gone.

The king sent his men to find Aladdin. They pulled him from his horse and took him to the king.

"Where is the princess?" cried the king.

"She is at home," Aladdin replied.

"But your home is gone," said the king. "Bring the princess back or you must die."

Aladdin could not get his lamp
because his house had gone,
so he rubbed his magic ring.

"Take me to the princess," said
Aladdin to the slave of the ring.

Suddenly, he was in his house
with the princess. She told him
about the old man with the lamps.

"That man is a wicked magician,"
said Aladdin. "I must get the lamp
back from him quickly!"

He gave the princess a little bag
and said to her, "Ask the magician
to supper. When he is not looking,
empty this into his cup."

The princess did as she was told,
and the magician fell back dead.

Aladdin picked up the lamp and rubbed it. When the slave appeared, Aladdin ordered, "Take us, and our home, back to where it was before."

The king looked out of the palace window. "The princess and Aladdin are back!" he said to the queen. They rushed to see the princess.

"I am so glad to be back," she cried.

"A wicked magician took me away but he is dead now. Dear Aladdin found me. I love him very much and you must love him, too."

The king and queen agreed to do so, and they all lived happily ever after.

A History of
Aladdin

The story of *Aladdin* is taken from
a collection of stories called
The Thousand and One Nights. These
stories are based on ancient Persian,
Arabian and Indian tales handed down
by word of mouth for hundreds of years.
They first appeared in their present
form, in Arabic, in 1450. The tales are
linked together by the story
of Sheherazade.

Sheherazade was the wife of the sultan
and had been condemned to death for
her wickedness. She managed to put
off her death by telling one of the
stories to her sister each night, in the
presence of the sultan. Being a very
clever woman, as well as a talented
storyteller, Sheherazade always left

the most exciting part of the story until
the following night. The sultan could
not bear to miss the end of each story,
and kept on putting off her death.

For a thousand and one nights
Sheherazade kept the sultan spellbound
with the stories. He eventually realized
that he had been wrong and forgave her.

Ladybird's 1975 retelling by
Marie Stuart helped to bring *Aladdin*
to a new generation of readers.

Collect more fantastic

LADYBIRD 🐞 TALES

Little Red Riding Hood
9781409311126

Goldilocks and the Three Bears
9781409311119

Cinderella
9781409311072

Jack and the Beanstalk
9781409311102

The Gingerbread Man
9781409311096

The Three Little Pigs
9781409311089

The Three Billy Goats Gruff
9781409311065

Hansel and Gretel
9781409311133

Puss in Boots
9781409311225

Rapunzel
9781409311195

Rumpelstiltskin
9781409311164

The Elves and the Shoemaker
9781409311188

Snow White and the Seven Dwarfs
9781409311171

The Enormous Turnip
9781409311218

The Magic Porridge Pot
9781409311201

Sleeping Beauty
9781409311157

The Princess and the Frog
9780718192556

Dick Whittington
9780718192532

The Big Pancake
9780718192549

Beauty and the Beast
9780718192587

The Little Red Hen
9780718192525

The Ugly Duckling
9780718193133

The Princess and the Pea
9780718192570

Chicken Licken
9780718192563

The Emperor's New Clothes
9780723271048

The Little Mermaid
9780723271055

Pinocchio
9780723271062

Aladdin
9780723271079

Endpapers taken from series 606d,
first published in 1964

A catalogue record for this book is available from the British Library

Published by Ladybird Books Ltd
80 Strand London WC2R 0RL
A Penguin Company

001

ISBN: 978-0-72327-107-9

Printed in China